First published in 2013
by Wayland

Text copyright © Anne Rooney
Illustration copyright © Ann Johns

Wayland
338 Euston Road
London NW1 3BH

Wayland Australia
Level 17/207 Kent Street
Sydney, NSW 2000

Series Editor: Louise John
Cover design: D.R.ink
Design: Lisa Peacock
Consultant: Shirley Bickler

A CIP catalogue record for this book is available from the British Library.

ISBN 9780750268714

Printed in China

Wayland is a division of Hachette Children's Books,
an Hachette UK Company

www.hachette.co.uk

Archie and Terrible Trevor

Written by Anne Rooney
Illustrated by Ann Johns

WAYLAND

"Dad, please can Izzy stay for tea?" Lucy said. "She's hungry."

Dad set a place for Izzy.

"I'm not sitting next to Invisible Izzy," Awful Archie said. "She's not real."

"Yes, she is!" shouted Lucy.

Dad put sandwiches and cake on Archie and Lucy's plates. He gave Izzy some, too.

Archie gobbled up his cake.
"Izzy hasn't eaten her cake,"
he said. "Can I have it?"
"She's saving it," Lucy said.

Lucy went to the kitchen to get
a drink. Archie ate Izzy's cake.

"Where's Izzy's cake gone?"
Lucy cried.

"She ate it," Archie said.
"No, she didn't," said Lucy.
"You ate it!"

"I did not!" Archie shouted.
"If Izzy is real, then maybe
Izzy ate it?"

"Be quiet, Archie," Dad said.

The next day, Archie told Mum Trevor was coming for tea.

"You don't know anyone called Trevor," Lucy said.

Dad set a place for Trevor.
"That's silly!" shouted Lucy.
"Trevor isn't real."

"I really hope Trevor and Izzy
are going to eat their tea,"
said Mum.

Archie ate Trevor's cake.
Then he ate Izzy's cake.

"Dad!" Lucy shouted. "Archie
ate Izzy's cake again!"
"I did not," Archie said.
"Trevor ate it."

Lucy went to find Dad.
Archie flicked Izzy's sandwich.
He pushed over her drink.

Dad and Lucy came back.
"Archie!" Dad said. "What is
this mess?"

"It wasn't me," Archie said.
"Trevor did it!"

Dad sent Archie for a bath.
A lot of water came out of
the bath and went on the
floor. Dad was cross.

"Trevor did it," Archie said.
"He hates baths."

At bedtime, Trevor would not turn the light off.

He would not stop playing Archie's trumpet.

Dad was very cross.
"It's not me!" Archie said.
"It's Trevor."

Archie would not get dressed in the morning. "Trevor has hidden my clothes," he said.

In the kitchen, Archie put
sweets into a bowl.

"Trevor likes sweets for
breakfast," Archie said.

"Archie," Dad said. "Trevor is terrible. He has to go."
"No!" shouted Archie. "Lucy has Invisible Izzy. It's not fair!"

"Trevor is not real," said Mum. "Yes, he is!" Archie said, pretending to cry.

Lucy started to cry, too.
"What's wrong?" Dad asked.

"Trevor is pulling Izzy's hair,"
she said. "Make him go away."

"No, he's not!" shouted Archie.
"You can't see Trevor! Or Izzy!"

"Archie," Mum said.
"Trevor must go. Trevor must
go because he's much
too naughty."

"Where will he go?" Archie asked. Mum opened the front door. "He can go in that taxi," she said.

"What taxi?" Archie said. "There's nothing there."

"There is," Mum said. "It's an invisible taxi."
"Goodbye, Trevor," Dad said.

"Hello, Ben," Archie said.

Mum looked surprised.
"He just got out of the taxi,"
said Archie. "He's my new
invisible friend."

"Oh, Archie!" said Dad. "You
are awful!"

START READING is a series of highly enjoyable books for beginner readers. The books have been carefully graded to match the Book Bands widely used in schools. This enables readers to be sure they choose books that match their own reading ability.

Look out for the Band colour on the book in our Start Reading logo.

The Bands are:

Pink Band 1

Red Band 2

Yellow Band 3

Blue Band 4

Green Band 5

Orange Band 6

Turquoise Band 7

Purple Band 8

Gold Band 9

START READING books can be read independently or shared with an adult. They promote the enjoyment of reading through satisfying stories supported by fun illustrations.

Anne Rooney has written lots of books for children including the All About Henry stories for this series. Have a look! She lives in a state of chaos with her two daughters, a tortoise called Tor2 and a blue lobster called Marcel.

Ann Johns likes to draw life – busy, lovely life. Birds flying, dogs jumping, people dancing... So always have a pencil handy, because you never know what exciting thing is waiting around the corner for you to draw!